MORE IN-THE-BAG STORIES

OBJECT TALKS FOR CHILDREN

BY

LOUISE KOHR

STANDARD
PUBLISHING
Cincinnati, Ohio

ISBN 0-87403-921-5
Copyright © 1992, The STANDARD PUBLISHING Company,
Cincinnati, Ohio
A division of STANDEX INTERNATIONAL Corporation.
Printed in U.S.

Contents

Introduction

These stories have an object or objects in a paper bag to use in telling the stories. They help hold children's interest and attention in these days of visual communication. The objects are easily obtainable at home or from a local discount store.

These stories were written for children's church or the children's time at the regular worship service.

A good story is a good story wherever it's told. These in-the-bag stories have a point children will be able to grasp, and they will not be entirely lost time for the adult listener.

The eight-year-old child is the median age targeted by the author. You may have to simplify the stories or raise them to the general level of your group. You should know better than anyone else the abilities of your listeners. These stories are merely outlines to follow.

If toddlers fail to understand, they will still benefit from sitting and listening to the worship service. Never underestimate a child's understanding, even though he or she may seem to be concentrating more on climbing the pulpit.

I hope you will find inspiration as you work with one of the most important segments of the church with these stories. The telling of them to children is a priceless privilege. Treasure it.

Creation

empty bag

(Put your hand in the bag and hold it out empty to the children. Say,) "What have I in my hand?"

"Nothing? Nothing, you say?"

One of the greatest stories from the Bible is the one about how God created a wondrous world out of nothing. The Bible says, "The earth was empty and had no form."

And God divided it into darkness and light, night and day; into earth and sky and sea. And when He had made it, He made it beautiful.

Creation is too wonderful to think about. Your mind gets all mixed up even trying to imagine how it could have happened.

Can you think of something God created from nothing? (mountains, seas, sun, moon, stars, lakes, trees, animals and birds, etc.)

Can anyone tell me how long it took God to create the world? Six days, our Bible tells us.

Sometimes when we are in a hurry to make something, we throw it together and let it go at that. God didn't do it that way. All He did He pronounced "good." And though He might let us help by planting seeds and tucking grass and leaves about the roots to keep them warm in winter, it was God who made the seeds, made the leaves to fall, the grass to grow.

Why did God take such care in all that He did to make the world so beautiful? It was because He loved us. He loves us still. When He had created the world, He said, "Here it is. I made it for you. Take care of it."

When you look about and see something beautiful in the world, remember it is a gift to us, all done up in love, and tied with rainbow hued ribbons.

> "God looked at everything he had made, and it was very good" (Genesis 1:31).

God's Day

string tied around finger

Now why did I tie this string round my finger? Sometimes people tie strings around their fingers to help them remember something. They look at their finger, see the string, and say, "O, yes, I remember . . ."

To remember the Sabbath is one of the special laws God gave His people. It is one of the Ten Commandments.

How did you remember that today was Sunday? Do you do anything special on Saturday to help get ready for Sunday? Does your mother have to remind you it is Sunday? Does she have to tie a string around her finger? Do you remember every Sunday? It pleases God when you remember His day.

He set us an example. He worked six days creating the earth. On the seventh day He rested. He is all wisdom and knew that if we worked every day, we should become too tired to enjoy the beautiful world He gave us.

What else should we do on Sunday? We should praise and thank Him. Of course, we should also do that on other days. But we should give Him special praise on His day.

Can you do this without going to church? Yes, but it is better there. He has said, "If two or three people come together in my name, I am there with them" (Matthew 18:20). So we are sure God is here. And we are gathered together with others who love Him.

I do have this string around my finger. I wonder whether I am forgetting something important, like maybe telling someone I love him. Of course, there is nothing so important as to tell God we love Him. People who remember God's day, to keep it holy, are happy people.

See you next Sunday when you remember it is His day, and come to worship and to praise Him.

"Remember to keep the Sabbath as a holy day" (Exodus 20:8).

Invitation

envelope

What have we here? It might be an invitation to a party.

Parties are special fun. *(You may want to open a large box and let loose some balloons.)* I wonder if Jesus celebrated birthdays when He was a child.

When you are invited to a party, do you feel excited and have a hard time waiting for the day of the party? And if someone has a party and you aren't invited, then how do you feel?

Party invitations are different. Some may have clowns on them, and some may have birthday candles. But they all say, "Come."

Come is a lovely word. It means you are wanted. It means "we want you." We should try to be the kind of boys and girls others will want to come to their party.

Can you tell me of a time when Jesus said "Come" in a special invitation to children? (Mark 10:14; Luke 18:16)

Come is a word used over and over in the Bible. The Bible says "When you are afraid, come and I will take away your fear." "Come when you are troubled, and I will help you." "Come when you are lonely and I will make you glad."

The invitation of Jesus is for every day in the week.

When you go to a party, you usually take a present. What do you have to give to Jesus? Happiness comes to those who give Him their heart.

We celebrate Jesus' birthday in December, but His invitation to come is for His children, old and young alike. Although the invitation may be especially for those who are young for He needs helpers, and children often have special gifts of sharing like smiles and hugs and love.

Come, let us sing! Come, let us be glad! Come, let us make a joyful noise unto the Lord!

"Come. My Father has given you his blessing" (Matthew 25:34).

9

Seeds

two or three apples
paring knife

No, we aren't going to make apple pie this morning. We are going to explore the inside of an apple to observe one of the small wonders of God's great world.

Did you ever cut an apple in two and observe the pattern in its heart? *(Cut the apples crosswise into halves and pass them around for all the children to see.)*

Is there a neatly arranged pattern of four seeds in your apple? Is there one in yours? In all the millions, billions and trillions of apples God has made through the passing years, there is this neat little arrangement of four seeds.

Each of these seeds if planted and nurtured will grow into an apple tree. Some seeds will grow nearby, where they fall; some may be used to plant new orchards; and still some may be carried in the craws of birds to far away places. From them will grow trees for beauty, shade, apple wood, and apple pies.

Now let's talk about the seeds of love in our hearts being like the seeds of the apple tree. The love seeds in our hearts will bear fruit as the apple tree bears apples. We need to share the seeds of love and kindness with everyone.

An apple orchard abloom in the spring is beautiful to see and gives the promise of much fruit. The farmer tends his orchard with care. Let us, like the farmer, tend carefully the seeds of kindness God has put into our hearts. There are many people all around us who need the love Jesus has planted in our hearts. He wants us to share this love.

Think about this, too. An apple pie bubbles with the love of the family who enjoys it, the person who baked it and God who gave us the apples.

"The seed is God's teaching" (Luke 8:11).

Roots

seed
rock

What have we here? A seed and a rock.

Which of the two would you say is the stronger?

Once we had a water pipe that began to leak. I called the repair man and he dug down and found that a root (from a seed) had grown right into that pipe and split it.

Sometimes roots (from a seed) can grow into brick walls and topple them. A seed can be stronger than stones.

You know something else? Seeds of love planted in hearts ready to receive them can be stronger than rocks. Rocks don't grow. They just lie there. But seeds grow. A seed of love, planted in the heart may grow into something big, like a church, or a hospital or a school.

A seed can grow into a book that will teach many about God. A seed can grow into a tree that will build a house.

Oh, there is no end to the good things that can grow from a seed planted in a heart.

Jesus told his disciples a story about seeds once. He told them ·that a seed planted in the heart that is ready for it, will grow and bear fruit, but wither and die in soil not prepared for it.

And so we come to church on Sunday to prepare our hearts for the seed God has ready to plant.

> "But what is the seed that fell on the good ground? That seed is like the person who hears the teaching and understands it" (Matthew 13:23).

Wrong Way

wing feathers from a goose

Can you tell me what these are?

Feathers, yes.

Can you tell me what kind of feathers?

They are goose feathers.

They are gray to match the early morning sky. Bright red geese might have been pretty, but gray feathers are probably safer from the hunter's guns.

Geese are strong, flying birds. They can travel for thousands of miles. They keep slugs out of farmer's gardens, and are sometimes kept for watchdogs. They make an awful rumpus if someone is prowling around at night.

They are faithful birds. Once Mr. Goose chooses a wife, he stays with her all his life. Sometimes a goose will grieve himself to death when he loses his mate.

One beautiful morning, I went outside on my way to work, and lo, there was a flock of geese flying over. But they were flying in the wrong direction. They were headed east, right out over the ocean. If they thought they were going south as they were supposed to be doing with winter coming on, then they were going to be surprised to find themselves in China.

I cupped my hands around my mouth and yelled to them. I waved my hands and tried to point them in the right direction. But they kept right on going east.

Sometimes we are like those silly birds. We get headed in the wrong direction, and it takes a lot to get us turned back in the way we should go. Wrong habits are stronger than the winds of the sky.

We need to ask God to help us get back in the way we should go. He will if we ask.

"Trust the Lord with all your heart" (Proverbs 3:5).

Shining for Jesus

light bulb

Good morning, children. God is glad to see you here in His house of worship today. Do you feel gladness in your heart?

Let's see, what have we in the bag today?

What is it? A light bulb. I don't see any light. Oh, it has to be hooked to the power to make it shine. That's right. Without power it is just glass and metal.

Before light bulbs were invented, we had lamps with smokey chimneys. Before that, we had oil flickering in little saucers, and before that we had candles. Now we have bulbs that turn on with a switch. But always we have had Jesus, who said, "You are the light that gives light to the world" (Matthew 5:14).

But just as the bulb has to be hooked into the power to show light, you have to be hooked into God's power to shine.

When I was a child, we used to sing a little song at Sunday worship that went like this:

"This little light of mine,
I'm going to let it shine,
Let it shine, let it shine."

Do we sing that song anymore? Do you know it? Do you shine for Jesus?

How do we get hooked up to God's power so we can shine for Him? One way is by coming to church school. Another is reading your Bible. Most of all, it is by talking to God in prayer, and in trying to be more like Jesus every day. The more we learn about Him, the more we love Him, the more we pray, the more like Him we will be.

God who gives the light expects you to let it shine.

"You are the light that gives light to the world" (Matthew 5:14).

Fives

glove

What is this? A glove, yes, and how many fingers does it have? Five! Why? Because God gave us five fingers. How would we have learned to count without fingers? We can count how many days until our birthday or how many days until Christmas?

God thought five fingers would work better than six. Six would have looked funny, and maybe we couldn't tie our shoes with only four.

God gives us what is best for us.

Five years old is a very important age. A five-year-old is full of questions. Why? Why? Why? Why guys are wise guys. It is also at this age that you start to school. Starting to school is a sign you are growing up.

Five is an important number in the Bible. God made the stars to have five points. David picked up five smooth stones when he went out to fight Goliath, the giant. And there were five loaves of bread in the basket from which Jesus fed the five thousand.

The white pine tree stands straight and tall. Some Indian tribes believe that to be born beneath a white pine will help you to be like the Great Spirit. The white pine has five needles on each frond. God keeps track of the sparrows that fall, and of the number of needles on the white pine. What a wonderful God He is. Can you imagine Him saying, "That will do?" No, what God does, is perfect.

We have five fingers on each hand to do kindly deeds. Five needles on every frond for beauty and fragrance. Thank You, God, for five fingers.

> "He took the five loaves of bread and the two fish. Then he looked to heaven and thanked God for the food" (Matthew 14:19).

Animals

animal crackers

(You may want to pass these and let each child take one. Be sure there are enough if you do this.)

God made the animals, and what a variety He made. Can you imagine what this world would be like if there were no animals only men? He made all animals from the tiny ant to the monstrous big animals. From twinkly little tail-wagging creatures to the lumbering beasts of the ocean, jungle, and mountains God created them. What fun God must have had creating so many different animals.

Each had its own place to fill, its own thing to do, just as you and I do.

God gave each kind of animal a different sound to make. Some animals cheep, some squeak, some roar and rumble. But God in His heaven, created He them.

What a wonderful God we have. Having created them, he had to produce the kind of food each would eat, the carnivorous meat eaters, the cud chewers, the whale, largest of animals which eats plankton, the tiniest of "lunches."

God did not create anything for "nothing", though I for one, would like to know what the pesky mosquito is for, unless it is to become a tasty snack for birds of the air.

So surely if God has a purpose for all of these, He has a special purpose for the "animal" made in His image–you and me.

How are you planning to serve Him? What are you hoping to become? If you don't know, you should talk it over with God through prayer. Ask for His guidance and then, stand by, listen for His answer.

> "There is a right time for everything. Everything on earth has its special season" (Ecclesiastes 3:1).

Change

bulb
flower

Know what this is? Who can change a bulb into a *(flower)*?

The world is full of change. Let us look at my watch. Will it be the same tonight as it is now? No, as the sun changes its place in the sky, the hands on my watch will change places on its face, marking the change of time.

Can you think of something else that changes? *(Examples: seasons, sky, trees, moon.)* The world changes with the seasons, snow for winter, daffodils and apple blossoms for spring, roses for summer, colorful leaves for fall.

It is God's plan that there should be change.

Do you know something else that changes every day? You! You change in the way God means for you to, in size, in knowing, and in becoming a little more like Jesus every day. The Bible says the boy Jesus grew in stature (that's big), in knowledge and in favor with God and man.

Can you tell me what dough changes into if you put it in a warm oven? *(Bread or cookies, maybe.)*

What an egg may change into if you put it under a hen? What a tadpole turns into? A seed? What can a worm change into?

If you care for a baby and love it, what will it change into? One of God's children like you.

Change is life. When the weather changes, we know God is in His heaven, looking after His world.

But there is one thing that never changes. Do you know what it is? It is God. He is the same yesterday, today, and forever. We can count on Him to remain true to His word. He is God, the Creator, the all Holy One.

In Malachi 3:6 we read "I am the Lord. I do not change."

> "Jesus Christ is the same yesterday, today, and forever" (Hebrews 13:8).

Promises

Bible
small bottle of seeds

What are these? Yes, seeds. Did you ever think of every seed as being a promise? It will grow into a tree, a flower, or a vegetable.

Can you keep a promise? It's hard sometimes, isn't it?

What is a promise? It is an agreement. It is saying you will (or won't) do something. And then sticking to your word no matter what. Sometimes it's something so exciting you feel you must share it or burst.

Baptism is a promise. You are promising to live the way God wants you to live and God is promising to guide you and help you.

Without promises this would be an unhappy world. Our Bible *(Pick it up.)* is full of promises. Because of God's promises we need not fear. He has promised to be with us. There will be a new day tomorrow. God never breaks His promises. He has promised to love us, no matter how many times we make mistakes. But He feels very sorry if we forget to tell Him we love Him, too.

One of the greatest promises ever known comes in bright colors. What is it?

The rainbow! God once destroyed His people with a flood, and He has set the rainbow in the sky as a promise that He will never do that again.

If you want to be happy, promise to do what He wants you to do, and to be what He wants you to be. Our loving Father will help you to grow stronghearted enough to keep your promise.

"I am putting my rainbow in the clouds. It is the sign of the agreement between me and the earth" (Genesis 9:13).

Children

Bible
book of Bible stories for children

Do you have a book of children's Bible stories with pictures in it?

Can anyone tell me a favorite children's story from it? Is it the story about what Jesus said when the disciples tried to send the little children away? I thought it might be because it is probably the favorite children's story in the Bible. What did He say?

You've heard the words many times.

There is another Bible story you don't hear so often. But I want you to hear these words, because they are very important. Jesus needed help to teach the people about God, His Father, and He chose twelve helpers to train. One day two of them got into an argument, and they came to Jesus for an answer.

He called a child and set him up in the midst of His helpers, and He said, "You must change and become like little children. If you don't do this, you will never enter the kingdom of heaven" (Matthew 18:3).

This is what I want to talk to you about. He was telling these grown-ups that He wanted them to be like children. Of course, sometimes children fail to be what He wants them to be, too. What He was saying was that children can be kind; they can be unselfish; they can be joyful; they can be loving. He wants all His followers to be like this.

Always remember, grown-ups may be watching you, so they can grow to be like Jesus wants them to be. He wants you to be a good example to them. Had you ever thought of that? Jesus is counting on you. Remember that.

> "Let the little children come to me" (Luke 18:16).

Hurts

adhesive bandage

Good morning.

What is this?

Does your mother have some of these? Does she ever use one on you? Do you cry when you are hurt? Everyone does sometimes!

There are lots of hurts in the world. We do not know why. God doesn't want it to be so. He is a loving God.

There are two kinds of hurts. There are outside hurts, for example when you cut your finger or toe or a bee stings you. You apply medicine or a bandage on these.

But there is another kind of hurt–inside hurt. For example if you wanted to go somewhere and your mother wouldn't let you. Or maybe when you got scolded for something you didn't do or maybe a friend was unkind. These are inside hurts, and bandages won't help them.

What do you do for inside hurts? You talk to Jesus about them. He understands. Once He was a child like you and He knows how it feels to hurt. When He grew up, He had more hurtful things than we will ever know. He will help you if you ask Him.

We used to have a child in the family. When he had an outside hurt and had been kissed and a bandage put on it, he would say: "It's all better now."

Jesus loves us. He doesn't want us to hurt. If you ask Him, He will make your hurts "all better."

"Give all your worries to him, because he cares for you" (1 Peter 5:7).

Little Things

candle, cup,
stamp, acorn

Little things can be big.

Babies are little, but they are sweet, aren't they?

What is this? A cup isn't very big, but a cup full of water can save the life of someone lost in the desert. Did you know you can live longer without something to eat than you can without water? Jesus said you show your love for Him by sharing a cup of cold water with someone in need.

A candle is small, but it can light up a dark room.

Know what this is? It is an acorn, but it can be lunch to a hungry squirrel. And it can grow into a mighty oak tree.

A star isn't small, but, to us, it looks small in the sky at night. It can remind us of God's love watching over us while we sleep.

What is this? A stamp. It isn't very big, but if you lick it and stick it on a letter, it can carry a message to someone who may be lonely.

A smile is not big, but it will stretch and stretch. A hug is not large, but you can show a lot of love with one.

A whisper is so small you can barely see or hear it. But it can make a big difference when you whisper "I love you" in someone's ear.

You are not so small anymore. You are bigger than you were last week, and you have a heart full of love to share. God is counting on you to share it.

When we talk to God, we can thank Him for loving us so much. We will be happy to do what we can to show His love.

"Whoever accepts a little child in my name accepts me" (Matthew 18:5).

Shining

flashlight

What is this? Yes, a flashlight.

Why do we have flashlights? What are they good for? They are for helping us find things in the dark.

Can anyone tell me why Jesus is like a flashlight?

He helps us to find what we are looking for.

There are lots of dark corners in the world. Do you know why? Because of people who do not let Jesus light their way. He helps us to find what we are looking for.

What are we looking for? We are looking for happiness and peace and love, and we will find them if we follow the light of Jesus. He shines His flashlight into corners where there is unkindness or anger or selfishness. God does this because He wants us to be happy. He wants us to share our happiness with others.

How do you make the flashlight work? You have to turn it on, don't you? *(Turn it on.)* How do you turn on the flashlight of Jesus' love? Can anyone tell me that?

Yes, through prayer. What is prayer? It is just talking to Jesus. It is asking Him to shine His light on us, and all who do not know Him. Let Him shine His flashlight into any dark corners you do not understand.

"I am the light of the world" (John 8:12).

God's Gifts

flower
butterfly
songbook

What have we in the bag? Joy makers.

In the early days of our country, there were few books, few schools, and no libraries. Lots of children attended school for only a short time, and many who lived in wooded or far out places, didn't go at all.

Much of what children learned, they learned from storytellers, parents or grandparents. Blessed was the child with grandparents who had a good supply of stories.

God loved His children and He wanted to give them joy. So He gave them flowers, skies, mountains, birds and butterflies to enjoy. He gave them music, the song of wind in the treetops, of birds and mother's lullabies to bring joy to their ears.

Flowers bring joy not only to the eyes, but the nose and to the bees. Wondrously was the world made by Him. Animals "see" with their noses. Did you ever "see" cookies baking? Did you ever touch the softness of clouds with your fingertips? Did you ever "see" the song of spring with your eyes?

Indian children were taught by storytellers. Some of the stories they were told were very beautiful. They learned through them to praise their god, the Great Spirit, and they never harmed one of His animals uselessly.

Joy is like jam. It has to be spread, and children are great spreaders. Spreading joy was an important job the children did.

God's world can, at times, get a little mixed up, but it is beautiful. You children are spreaders of joy. Share its beauty with all through songs and hugs and kindly deeds.

Joy, music, laughter, birds, flowers, and kindly words worn on smiling faces are a few of God's wonderful gifts.

"Serve the Lord with joy. Come before him with singing" (Psalm 100:2).

22

Music Maker

flute

(You may have to import a flute player for this one. I did.)

Good morning, Children. Today I brought something special to share with you. Can anyone guess what is in this thin black case? Right. It's a flute, a music maker.

Now I will have it play a tune for you. *(Take flute out of case.)* "Okay flute, play!" I don't hear anything. Why doesn't it play? Oh, it has to be put together first. Right, it has to be ready before it can make music. *(Put the flute together, then hold it up for the children to see.)*

"Okay, flute. Now, play!" It still isn't making any music. Why isn't my flute playing? Someone has to do his part. Someone has to blow into my flute to make music.

(Blow into it. Play a short tune, preferably something familiar to the children, such as "Jesus Loves Me.")

God loves music. He has given us many instruments and helpers to play them. What makes the sound coming from the instrument? Breath or wind going through the flute makes the flute live.

Boys and girls, God has promised to give us the Holy Spirit to teach us and to be a friend to us. He has promised to live within our hearts if we ask Him in. The word for spirit in the Bible is "wind." God's wind blowing through us makes music. We don't have to sound like a flute, of course. We can make God's music in many ways such as with smiles, kind words, good deeds, and singing.

The birds, the wind, water trickling over rocks in the brook, and you help to make this a more beautiful world.

"You should know that you yourselves are God's temple. God's Spirit lives in you" (1 Corinthians 3:16).

Be's

long paper that unfolds to show a string of B's

Good morning. Can you tell me what buzzes? What are these? *(Unfold the paper.)*

I don't hear any buzzing.

One of the wonders in God's world is the busy little bee. It has a task to do in this world and it doesn't waste any time. In feeding itself, it carries pollen to trees and flowers and grains. If the bees didn't do this, the plants would not grow.

The bee can travel long distances. Its eyesight is not very good, so God made the flowers different colors, not only to make them beautiful but so the bees could find them.

A bee will go back to the same flower again and again until all the nectar has been taken from it. If God can use a little bee to make this a better world, of course, He has use for you.

Bees are only mentioned a couple of times in the Bible, but there are mentions of honey and of lands flowing with milk and honey as being good lands.

Now let's "buzz" a little about bees. As you grow, you will ask yourself, "What will I **B** when I grow up? Will I **B** a minister, a doctor, a teacher? Will I **B** a builder or a farmer?"

There is one thing you can **B** sure of.

God will always **B** near, and He will **B** willing to help you to **B** whatever you want to **B**. **B** sure to ask His guidance.

"You know him. He lives with you and he will be in you" (John 14:17).

Toys and Batteries

toy that runs with a battery

(Wind up the toy and set it going. Hold up the battery.) Can you tell me what this is? Yes, a battery.

What do you suppose your grandparents played with when they were children? They didn't have batteries in those days.

Your grandparents or great-grandparents probably had rag dolls with shoe-button eyes and yarn hair and cradles made of wood for the girls. The boys may have had a bow and arrow, or they may have fashioned noise-making toys or a whistle made from willow branches.

(Start the battery toy running again.)

What do you do when your toy stops running? Yes, you set it to running again. When the battery wears out, you have to have a new battery.

We are like toys that run down. When trouble comes and things go wrong, we need to turn to God to be recharged. We do this through prayer to set our lives right again.

We have to ask God. God knows our needs and He is ready and faithful to get us going again–if we ask. To remember this is like knowing a toy will run smoothly again with a new battery in it. So will our lives run smoothly again if we let God recharge us.

"Continue to ask, and God will give to you" (Matthew 7:7).

Be Glad

frowning/smiling face

"Hello! Oh, I'm sure he would. I'll tell him. He'd love it. Thank you."

"That was Aunt Ruthie. She asked if you would like to go to the zoo with her on Saturday."

Would he? Danny loved going to the zoo. And he loved going places with his Aunt Ruthie. She was fun. He could hardly wait for Saturday. But early Saturday morning the telephone rang again .

"Yes, I'll tell him," Mother said.

"Aunt Ruthie says she has company. She won't be able to go to the zoo today. She will take you on another day soon."

Danny didn't want to go to the zoo another day. He wanted to go that day. His mother saw how disappointed he was. She reminded him, "There are those books we got at the library the other day."

"I don't want to read," Danny said. *(Show picture sad side up.)*

"Then we'll make grandma happy by writing her a letter."

"I don't want to write a letter," Danny said.

"Then call Jeannie and ask her to come over to play."

"I don't want to play with Jeannie," Danny told his mother.

He went out on the back step, put his chin in his hand, and felt sorry for himself. Pretty soon he felt something warm against him. It was his puppy, Muddle, wagging his tail in such a glad way it looked like two tails. But Danny only pushed him away and went on feeling sorry for himself. The sun came out. It was glad. A bird on a bush was singing its happiest song. It was glad. Suddenly Danny was ashamed of himself for being so grumpy. He got up and went inside and told his mother he was sorry he had been cross.

"That's my boy," mother said. "God gives us so many things to make us glad that it is really bad when we are sad." *(Smiling side up.)*

Would someone like to say why he is glad today?

> "I will be glad because of your love" (Psalm 31:7).

Family

picture of a family

(Explain that you can't see hugs, of course, but they are very important.)

God is a wonderful Father. He hugs us all the time. He hugs us by giving us blessings. He gives us more blessings than we can count on the fingers of our hands and our toes together. *(Hold up your hands so the children will hold up theirs.)* Yes, more than that.

He gives us beautiful things to see and eyes to see them.

He gives us music and happy sounds and ears to hear them.

He gives us hands and wants us to serve Him with them.

He gives us food and health so we can run and play.

One of the greatest of His gifts is a family to love us. He knows our needs and gives us mothers and daddies and brothers and sisters and other family members. The family that thanks Him, that worships Him, that comes together in His house to praise Him is a happy family.

God knew that living together in families was the way to happiness. But He expects you to do your part to make it a happy family, by being kind, by helping, by sharing. Don't forget that, will you?

Take your family a hug this morning. Tell them you love them.

"Whoever loves God must also love his brother" (1 John 4:21).

Salt

salt shaker

What is this?

A salt shaker. Right. Did you ever see your mother putting salt on something using one of these? Why did she do that?

Our bodies need salt. Salt makes food taste better. Animals need it too. Farmers provide salt blocks for their cows. Shepherds give it to their sheep.

The Bible speaks of salt a number of times. In Bible times, men dug salt from mines, packed it on their donkeys and went through villages selling it. Salt was found in hot, dry places, and the sun would bake the taste out of it. To find good salt, men had to dig under the dried out salt.

Jesus asks, "If the salt has lost its flavor," if it has been out in the sun too long, "What good is it?"

He compares eating food flavored with sun-burnt salt to living a life without prayer.

He also said "You are the salt of the earth." Just as salt makes food taste better, Jesus meant that those who love and obey God make the world better. We are His children, and we can make this a better world as He wants us to.

This is a parable-kind of story that Jesus told about little things that help us to understand bigger things.

Some people collect salt shakers. They are made in hundreds of different sizes and shapes. When you see a collection of them or one on the table, remember Jesus said, "You are the salt of the earth."

We bring joy, peace, love, and happiness to the world just as salt brings flavor to food.

"You are the salt of the earth" (Matthew 5:13).

Birds

picture of a bird

Hello. This morning, my good friends, I have a picture of a bird in my bag because I want to talk about birds.

What kinds of birds can you think of?

One of them woke me this morning, singing its heart out, praising God. Birds are special gifts to His children. We know He cares for them, and He sees each one that falls.

He made them to be beautiful and to sing. We can learn from them, too.

The sparrow teaches us to be helpful, flying about eating bugs that harm flowers and food and fruit.

The robin teaches happiness, hopping about looking for worms, showing its bright red breast on days that may be cold and wintry when the sun forgets to shine.

The meadowlark teaches thankfulness, announcing spring with happy notes telling everyone that winter is past and summer is coming.

The dove reminds us of love. Noah sent the dove out from the ark to find dry land. Wherever we see doves, we are reminded of the stable where the baby Jesus was born, where doves might have cooed in the rafters.

The eagle teaches us to be brave, soaring in the wind in high mountain places, trusting God.

God watches over the birds that bring joy to His children. I thought of these things this morning when I heard a bird sing. When you see or hear one, let it remind you to be helpful like the sparrow, happy like the robin, thankful like the meadowlark, loving like the dove, and brave like the eagle.

Let it make you think of God who cares for all.

"Then God said, . . . 'let birds fly in the air above the earth'" (Genesis 1:20).

God Needs You

empty purse

God made the heavens and the earth, the seas and all that in them is.

And everything He has made has a purpose in life.

All created things declare His glory.

Every bird that flies, every creature that moves and breathes has something to give.

Every leaf of the forest, every blade of grass is good for something. Every tree, bush, or vine gives. The flowers share their perfume and beauty. The sun gives light, the ocean receives streams from every land, and takes to give. Everything is a part of God's plan for sharing.

Someone listening to the story may ask, "Teacher, what does a mosquito have to give?"

The teacher may hesitate a moment. "Ask a bird," the teacher says. "The bird will tell you that a mosquito makes a lovely afternoon snack."

When Jesus sent the disciples out into the world to teach, He told them, "Take nothing with you, no bag, no money in your purse. Be shod with sandals and take only the clothes you are wearing."

Why do you think He told them that? I think it was because He wanted them to know that the greatest thing He could give anyone was love. It is still so today. The very best gift anyone has to offer the world is **love.**

The word love appears hundreds of times in our Bible. God wants you to know He loves you, and you can give love.

The most important words in all the world are these three, "God is love."

"God is love" (1 John 4:8).

30

Talent

picture drawn in bright crayon colors

Can anyone tell me what it means to have talent?

A talent is something you are able to do especially well. Maybe you can draw well, or you can sing better than some, or maybe you have a talent for helping others.

Talents are **gifts** from God. He needs helpers, and He wants those to whom He gives special gifts to use them for Him.

He gives the talent of speaking to the minister, the talent of singing to those in the choir, and the talent to play the organ to the organist.

But you don't have to use all talents in the church. The world needs talents just as the thirsty garden needs rain. Maybe your talent is loving others and being an example.

God has given everyone a talent, but you may not have discovered what yours is. Ask your parents or someone close to you what you do well, and then try to do it even better. Ask God what you can do to help make this a better world.

Talented people are happy people when they use their talents for God because giving makes us happy. That's why God gave us talents to share. They don't have to be big, but they will grow as we practice using them.

Talent is what Jesus gives us for giving, and little bursts of happiness are what makes life worth living.

Share your talent or gift with someone this week.

"Each person has his own gift from God" (1 Corinthians 7:7).

Puzzle

puzzle

What have we here?

A puzzle. That's right. Can you put puzzles together? Do you have some?

Living is like putting a puzzle together. Each day is a new day to fit into your life. Some pieces are easier to fit. Some go together more smoothly than others. But you can't fit a piece in where it doesn't belong, can you? No, all the pieces must fit together. And you can't finish your puzzle if there is a missing piece, can you?

It is easier to put a puzzle together if you have a picture pattern to follow. God gave us a pattern to follow in putting our lives together. This pattern is Jesus, His Son. He went about doing good, He taught us to say, "thank you" and to share.

Can you think of any other patterns He gave us to help put the puzzle of our lives together?

He taught us to love one another and to remember His day, to keep it holy.

If you are having trouble putting some of the pieces of your life together, what can you do? Turn to Jesus and ask Him to help. He is always near.

Each day is a new piece of the puzzle. This week we have seven new pieces to add to the puzzle of our lives. We have begun the week right by coming to His house to learn of Him. He is happy that we are here today, and He will be with us the rest of the week.

"Please remember me. You are my helper and savior" (Psalm 40:17).

Sharing

pictures of children sharing

Caring and sharing are twins. They go together like an ear on either side of your head.

If you care, you want to share. With whom do you share? When you are a baby you don't know anything about sharing. All babies know is getting—love, rest and care. They reach out to take food, playthings, brightly-colored toys. But as you grow, you learn to give as well as take. You learn to share your toys, snacks, love, and happiness.

Can anyone tell me why happiness is like a bad cold or the measles? You get one of them from someone, pass it on to another, and that person gives it to someone else. That is called contagious. Happiness is contagious, too.

Look about you and you will see that the happiest people are those who have learned to share. Do you think the boy who shared his lunch with the five thousand Jesus fed on the hillside that long ago day was happy?

Do you think the widow with her little bit of money was happy she shared what she had in the temple that day?

Jesus said, "It is more blessed to give than to receive" (Acts 20:35). Did you ever give your mother something and see how happy it made her?

God wants us to be happy. He gives us His love and many gifts every day. He wants us to share His love with others. In Hebrews 3:14 we read, "We all share in Christ."

"It is more blessed to give than to receive" (Acts 20:35).

Talk

telephone

What is this?

A telephone, yes, and what do you do with it?

You talk to your friends or maybe your grandparents on it.

Can you talk to God over the telephone?

No, you don't need a telephone to talk to God. God is nearer than the phone on the wall. He hears and answers when you call.

Parrots talk. Parents talk. The difference is, parrots talk with loud squawks. Parents talk with love. God talks with love. We talk to Him through prayer. The more you talk to Him, the more you know about love. It is good to be able to talk to God and to your parents and friends.

Sometimes something happens to children so that they cannot speak. Usually it is because they cannot learn words because they cannot hear. I read about a class for children who could not speak. They were happy, smiling children. They couldn't speak out loud, but they could talk. God loves you whether or not you can speak out loud.

Let me show you how they sang "Jesus Loves Me."

Nod head for "yes."

Point upward for "Jesus."

Cross arms over your heart for "loves."

Touch your own heart for "me."

Spread hands together like a book for "Bible."

Touch finger to lips for "tells."

Touch your heart for "me."

And clasp your hands together for "so."

Can you "sing" it with me, without words as the children who couldn't speak did? *(Sing it slowly.)*

He loves all children everywhere.

"When you talk, you should always be kind and wise" (Colossians 4:6).

Our Senses

picture of flower,
butterfly, bird
a songbook

Can anyone tell me what our senses are?

How many are there?

Can you name them?

(Take the pictures out of the bag.) God showed His love for us by creating many beautiful things. Can you name some of them? *(Show pictures.)* And He gave us eyes to see them.

(Take out the songbook.) God gave us ears to hear. He gave us music. We can hear the birds sing. There are all kinds of things to make music, like the harp David the shepherd boy played and the organ in our church. Wherever you go in the world, people make music. Some play on sticks or drums or pipes, and all manner of strange instruments.

There is a song that says: "For the beauty of the earth, for the glory of the skies. For the love which from our birth over and around us lies, Lord of all, to Thee we raise this our hymn of grateful praise." The third verse says, "For the joy of ear and eye."

God gave us noses to smell flowers or cookies baking.

He gave us the sense of taste to enjoy all the wonderful foods He made.

He gave us fingers to feel the softness of our kitten or a flower petal.

We can say "thank you" to God for our senses to enjoy all the wonderful things God gave us.

> "Serve the Lord with joy. Come before him with singing" (Psalm 100:2).

Leaves

handful of leaves

A leaf is one of the little things that God created, but it has a very important job in our world. What are leaves for?

They give us shade in summer. They soak up sun for nourishment and make food and send it to needy roots below ground and to the rest of the plant.

Trees are like God's calendar. When they begin to leaf out, we know that spring is on its way. When they are green and give us shade, we know it is summer. When they turn red and gold and begin to fall, it is a sign that winter is coming.

They keep us cool in summer, and I'm sure, are one of the reasons birds sing. Leaves furnish protected places among the branches for nest building.

Falling leaves help enrich the ground, and blanket flowers and growing things to protect them from the winter cold. They are a vital part of God's ecology. Does anyone know what that means? It is growing things and the elements, rain and sun and nature working together to make the world beautiful. It is like a puzzle. Each piece needs to fit.

When we burn wood to heat or light our homes, stores or churches, when we drive cars or machines with gasoline, it produces a poison gas called carbon dioxide. Leaves need this gas to live. They absorb this poison and give off oxygen which we need to live. Without leaves, there would come a time when we couldn't tolerate the carbon dioxide in the air. That is one reason we should take good care of our trees and plant others to take the place of those destroyed for wood or to make places for building new homes.

There are so many things, both big and little in this world God has created, that it is almost impossible to thank Him for all of them. But we can try.

"Then all the trees of the forest will sing for joy" (Psalm 96:12).

School

tablet
pencil
box of crayons
ruler or bottle of paste

What have we in the bag this morning? *(Show items.)* These are clues to what we are going to talk about. What do you suppose it is?

School. Right. We are going to thank God that we can go to school. In some parts of the world, children get to go to school for a short time, if at all. In the early days of our country, there were very few schools.

How many of you are starting first grade? Are you just a bit frightened about how things are going to be? Were you afraid when you went to kindergarten? Did your mother take you?

You aren't frightened anymore, are you?

Can you remember other times you were afraid? Do you often remember the verse about, "I will not be afraid because the Lord is with me."

Let me tell you a secret. Grown-ups sometime get frightened, too. They are afraid that someone may get sick, or maybe someone does get sick and they are afraid they may not get well. Or they may be afraid they won't be able to do a job that needs doing, or that they may have done something that displeased God.

What can you do when you are afraid? You can pray to God. You can ask God to help you. He is always ready and willing. He says, "They will call to me, and I will answer them" Psalm 91:15.

Remember, He is nearer to you than the new school sweater you will be wearing. Ask Him to help you trust Him, and stop being afraid.

"I will not be afraid because the Lord is with me" (Psalm 118:6).

Show and Tell

Bible

What is this? A Bible, yes. It is the show and tell book of life, the most important book in the world.

Do you have a show and tell day in your school?

Bible stories show us how to live so that we can tell others about Jesus. Some of these stories are parables. Para means "beside" so parables are "beside-stories." He told us stories about little things like sheep or seeds to make us understand about bigger things in life. He told us about seeds growing to help us understand about how love grows. He told us about the shepherd's love for his sheep, to help us see how much Jesus loves us.

There is a parable about a man going down a road through a rough country. He was struck down by robbers and left to die.

Another traveler came by that way. He saw the man in the ditch, but he walked by on the other side of the road. Another traveler came by, he went over and looked at the man then walked by on the other side of the road.

But the third traveler saw the man in the ditch and was sorry for him. He stopped and put oil on the man's wounds. Then he put him on his own donkey and took him to an inn where he gave the innkeeper money to pay for his care. He said that if that wasn't enough money, he would give him more when he came back that way.

Another name for parables could be "see-through" stories. You see through them some greater truths God wants you to understand.

Jesus wants us to show our love for Him by our lives and by what we do. He lived a see-through life so we might come to understand His love for us.

> "Love the Lord your God. Love him with all your heart, . . . soul, . . . strength, and all your mind" (Luke 10:27).

Crayons

box of regular crayons
box of jumbo crayons

How many colors are there in the regular school-size box of crayons? How many in the jumbo box?

Can you remember when you couldn't have crayons because you might eat them? And when you got old enough for them, did you ever color the wall, a book, or something you shouldn't? What happened, or would you rather not say?

Probably one of the first things you drew with your crayons was a rainbow. How many colors are there in a rainbow? When you draw a rainbow, do you remember God's promise?

What color would you use to draw the sun? The rain? The moon? The stars? Now here's a tough one. What color would you use to draw love? You can't show love on paper, except maybe in words.

What color would you draw a hug? Another word for hug is "embrace." It is in the Bible several times. The Bible says that on the day the disciples tried to send the children away, Jesus "took the children in his arms." Surely that means He hugged them.

What color would you use for lonely? Blue, perhaps? There are many lonely people in the world, some of them in your own town, neighborhood, maybe even in your own family.

There is a great shortage of smiles and hugs in the world. You can do something about that.

Color the world with the bright colors of happiness. Ask God to open your hearts and eyes to the needs of those about you. Don't forget to thank Him for the love, the family, and the friends that He has given you.

And when you give someone a hug, tell him it is not for him to keep but to give to someone else. That way the supply will grow.

"There is a time to hug" (Ecclesiastes 3:5).

The Shepherd

toy lamb or picture of a lamb

What is this? A lamb. God gives us lambs. The wool from these lambs gives us warm blankets and warm sweaters and mittens for school.

The Bible calls Jesus the Good Shepherd. We are His lambs.

Once there was a shepherd who sat on a stump in the sun, and he said to a child. "I wish I had been here when Jesus was. If I could have walked with Him, heard Him speak, and seen His face, then I would have been able to believe in Him."

The child said, "Come with me." And he took the shepherd by the hand. "Look about you," said the child, "and see Jesus in the beauty of His world.

"See Him in the brook that brings water to the meadow and to the thirsty animals.

"See Him in the sky, like a blue bowl turned upside down; in the clouds, in the trees, in the rainbow's arch, in a butterfly.

"Hear Him speak in the singing of birds, the laughter of children, the hum of bees gathering honey, the whisper of the wind.

"Feel His touch in the warmth of sunshine on your face."

The old shepherd looked at the world about him. A lamb with a waggly tail came to nuzzle at its mother. And in the love of the mother sheep for her lamb, he remembered the love of his own mother and he SAW Jesus.

He stooped and picked a white-petaled daisy, and holding it in his hand, he said, "Thank you, child, for opening my eyes. Though I cannot see Jesus, I see signs of His love wherever I look. I believe!"

"The Lord is my shepherd. I have everything I need" (Psalm 23:1).

40

Las Posadas

piñata

(You can use a piggy bank if a piñata is not available.)

In our country we celebrate some holidays: the birthdays of Lincoln, and Washington, the Fourth of July, and Thanksgiving that are special only to our country. Other countries have their own special holidays. But Christmas is celebrated everywhere. The Christ child came to all.

In Mexico, besides Christmas, the children celebrate the sixteenth day of December. It is called Las Posadas, which means "the inns." On that night, the children go from one home to another, searching for a place where the baby Jesus will be welcome.

Surely Christmas is a happy time all around the world, but Las Posadas, when the children seek permission to enter, reminds the people to make room in their hearts for the baby Jesus. It is a beautiful and happy custom.

Have you ever been to a piñata party? This is another Mexican custom. The piñata is made from paper or thin plaster and is made in the shape of a sheep, donkey, or some other animal. On Christmas Eve it is hung from the ceiling and is broken open by a stick in the hand of a blindfolded child. When it breaks open, candies and surprises fall out. Everyone scrambles for his share.

May you, too, find room for the Baby in your hearts.

"There were no rooms left in the inn" (Luke 2:7).

Love

Bible
flower
cookie

(Hold up Bible.)
What is this? The book that tells us of God's love, the Bible.
What is love?
It is warmth. It is joy. It is sharing.
Can you feel love?
When someone hugs you or gives you something to make you happy or says, "I'm sorry," you can feel love.
Can you touch it?
When you hold a baby in your arms or the sun shines warmly upon you or someone says, "I love you," you can feel love.
Can you smell it?
You can smell it in flowers *(Hold up flower and cookie.)* or in a pan of fresh cookies your mother has just baked for her loved ones.
Can you hear it?
You can hear it all about you. In the buzz of bees, in the "come walk with me's" and "thank you's" and in praises to God and the music of the universe.
Can you see it?
You can see love in the eyes of your mother or a friend. You can see it in the beauty of the world God has made, in flowers and trees and mountains. You can see it in the wagging of your dog's tail. You can see it wherever you turn.
God is love, and He is everywhere.

"I will praise you, Lord, with all my heart" (Psalm 9:1).

Joy

silver star

(Hold up the star.)

Our story this morning has been called the most beautiful story in the world. *(Lay down the star.)*

Each time I stop while I'm telling the story, hold up your hands and say "Joy." If it makes you feel especially joyful, say it twice.

Over two thousand years ago, a bright star appeared in the sky. **(Joy!)** Most of the people went their usual way, paying little, if any, attention to the star. But some astronomers saw it, and they said, "Let us follow and see where it leads." They got on their camels and traveled over the desert a long way to where the star stood over a house in Bethlehem. **(Joy!)**

Before this happened, there were shepherds, sleepy and tired, keeping watch over their flocks by night. Suddenly the sky was very bright and there was a heaven full of angels singing, "Glory to God in the highest. Peace on earth." **(Joy!)**

The shepherds said, "Let us go to Bethlehem and see what this singing is all about." **(Joy!)**

They left their flocks and went to the stable and found the Babe lying in the manger. **(Joy! Joy! Joy!)** It was God's Son, come to teach us to love one another.

We call this day Christ-mas Day, after God's Son. We celebrate this day by remembering Jesus and singing songs of praise.

Let us fold our hands together at this time. Let us bow our heads and say, "Joy! Joy! Joy!" softly. And then, because God gave us the Christ-mas Child, let us spread that joy, not just at this time of the year, but every day of our lives.

"I am bringing you some good news. It will be a joy to all the people" (Luke 2:10).

43

Blueprints

blueprints

Do you know what these are? *(Unfold them.)* They are blueprints.

Blueprints can be plans for building a house, a school, a church, or even a greenhouse. Every builder needs a set of directions.

A good builder wouldn't think of starting to build something without blueprints. All kinds of things could go wrong. He might run out of materials. He might end up with a chicken house. The doors might not open or close or the chimney might not stand straight or the foundation might not be strong.

Strong is a word loved by God. It is often used in the Bible. In Matthew 10:22 we read, "The person who continues strong until the end will be saved."

We are builders. The Bible calls our bodies temples of the Lord, and that calls for faith builders. The builder should know what he wants of life and whom he would serve.

Good builders should go to church and church school to study God's blueprints for life. Our building must have a strong foundation. If God blueprints it, then the walls will be straight and strong.

Remember the story in the Bible about the man who built his house on the sand and the man who built his house on the rock? When the rains came, the house built on the sand fell. But the house built on the rock stood firm and strong, because the man had blueprints approved by God.

"Your word is like a lamp for my feet and a light for my way" (Psalm 119:105).

Grandparents

pictures of grandparents

Some children are lucky because they may have as many as half-a-dozen grandparents and great grandparents.

Some children are lucky because they live near enough to their grandparents to see them often or even lucky enough to have a grandmother or grandfather living with them.

But others have to drive a long way or even fly in a plane to see their grandparents. They may even live in a country beyond the sea, and have to write them letters and not see them for long periods of time.

Grandparents are usually good storytellers because they have a lot of experience. Some grandparents are good cookie bakers. Most grandparents are good listeners. You are lucky if they live near you.

Having them near is nice, but if they live far away, it can help you to understand better about loving God. Though your grandparents may live a long way from you, you know they love you. That's the way it is with God. You do not see Him, but you can feel love. You know in your heart that He is there, loving you and watching over you. In the Bible God tells you He loves you. Just as you know your grandparents are loving you and telling you so, even though you do not see them often.

God is love and love goes everywhere.

> "Nothing can separate us from the love God has for us" (Romans 8:38).

Rainbow

streamers of rainbow-colored paper

(Hold up each streamer as you ask.) Tell me, what color is this?

Have you a favorite color? What fun God must have had mixing colors for the first rainbow!

(Take the streamers one at a time.) Take red, it is a joyful color, but it isn't a rainbow. It is only part of a rainbow.

Take blue. Without blue, what color would the sky be? We wouldn't have any bluebirds, forget-me-nots, or delphinium. But blue is not a rainbow in itself. It is only a part of a rainbow.

Take yellow for sunshine, daffodils, or sunflowers, or the green in the grass and trees. But yellow and green don't make a rainbow.

(Wave the colors.) It takes all of these to make a beautiful rainbow.

Our church is beautiful. It has different colors or parts as a rainbow.

It has a minister, choir, children, teachers, and congregation. But none of these by themselves make a church.

A clock won't keep time with just hands. A car won't run with just wheels. A school isn't a school with just teachers. A church isn't a church with just ministers.

It takes all of us doing our part to make a church a church, just as it takes all of these colors to make a rainbow.

"Christ gave each one of us a special gift" (Ephesians 4:7).

Image

hand mirror

(Have children look in the mirror and see their reflection/image.)

The Bible says we are created in the image of God.

That doesn't mean that when someone looks at us they will say: "Hey, you look like God."

No one has seen God.

But when they look at what we do and listen to what we say and know who we are, they will know that we are like Him in some ways, that we bear witness to Him.

When they see kindness or love reflected in us, that is what it means to say we are made in His image. If we are good as He is good, that goodness will show in us.

On the first page of our Bible, it says: "God created human beings in his image" (Genesis 1:27). For God is love. He wanted everyone to love, so He made us like himself. His love will be reflected in us if we try to be like Him.

We can't be like Him without love. If we love one another, it will show in our lives, in our faces.

We want kindness and love to be reflected in our faces when we look in the mirror.

Our prayer should be, "May I make my life an image of Yours. May my countenance glow with the light of Your love. Amen."

"God created human beings in his image" (Genesis 1:27).

Teacher Appreciation Day

Bible
red paper heart

Good morning, children.

"This is the day that the Lord has made. Let us rejoice and be glad today!"

Every day is His and every day is a day for rejoicing.

Today we want to give special thanks for His gift to us of teachers. They study, as the Bible tells us, "to show themselves approved" and come to church every Sunday to tell us about God's love and what He wants us to do for others.

Jesus said, "Let the children come unto me!" And we come to church school each week so that we may become more like Him.

As we come, He puts a song in our hearts to share with others.

Let us say,

"Thank You, God, for teachers to
teach us how to pray.
Thank You, for teachers to teach us
how to walk with You each day,
Thank You, God, for Jesus who was
a teacher, too.
Who came to teach
us how to be kind and true.
Thank you, teachers for the truth that
you impart.
Thank you, teachers, here is our heart."
(Hold up the red paper heart.)

"This is the day that the Lord has made. Let us rejoice and be glad today!" (Psalm 118:24).